IN EVERY BREATH

A STORY OF LOVE, STRENGTH, AND LETTING GO

MITESH HOOD

Made with ♥ on the Notion Press Platform
www.notionpress.com

To all those who face life's battles with courage and grace.
To the warriors living with invisible illnesses, who fight every day even when no one is watching.
To my family, for their unwavering support and love, reminding me that I am never alone.
And to those who stand by our side, offering strength when we have none left—
This book is for you.

Contents

Foreword

The journey of living with a chronic illness is one of unimaginable complexity, but also one of resilience, hope, and profound human strength. In this story, we explore the life of a woman who, despite being a doctor accustomed to saving others, finds herself confronted with a diagnosis that she cannot simply cure. Her battle with myasthenia gravis is a story of learning to cope, adapt, and ultimately thrive against the odds.

Through this novel, we are reminded of the incredible power of community, family, and the unshakable human spirit. It is not just a tale of one woman's struggle, but a universal reflection of the challenges faced by those living with chronic illnesses. The characters in these pages are not heroes because they are extraordinary in their abilities, but because they are ordinary people who continue to fight, to love, and to live despite the obstacles placed before them.

This book also shines a light on the often invisible emotional toll of illness, and how personal connections and support systems can make all the difference in navigating life's most difficult moments. It demonstrates the importance of empathy, not only from healthcare professionals but from friends, family, and even strangers who offer a listening ear.

As you turn these pages, you will witness a story of courage and vulnerability. You will see the highs and lows, the moments of despair balanced by moments of triumph. And, most importantly, you will come to understand that true strength is not defined by the absence of struggle, but by the ability to continue moving forward in the face of it.

This book is a tribute to those who live with chronic conditions, to the caregivers who stand by their side, and to the medical professionals who dedicate their lives to healing and understanding. It is a reminder that no one is alone in their journey.

I hope this story resonates with you as much as it has with me. It is not only a reflection of life's challenges, but also a celebration of life's possibilities.

— Mitesh Hood

PREFACE

In a world often defined by challenges and uncertainties, the story of Sarah, John, and Emily emerges as a poignant reminder of the strength of the human spirit. This novel, "In Every Breath: A Story of Love, Strength, and Letting Go," explores the intricate tapestry of love, loss, and resilience woven through the lives of a family grappling with the unrelenting challenges posed by a chronic illness—myasthenia gravis.

Sarah, a dedicated doctor, exemplifies unwavering courage as she confronts her own diagnosis, balancing her passion for healing others with the reality of her condition. Through her journey, we witness the dual struggle of maintaining her identity and the fear of becoming defined by her illness. This emotional exploration serves as a mirror reflecting the experiences of countless individuals facing their own battles against chronic diseases, offering readers a glimpse into the complexities of their lives.

As we follow John and Emily alongside Sarah, we delve into the depths of grief and the incredible power of hope. Their journey underscores the importance of support, understanding, and the enduring bonds of family. It is a celebration of life's fleeting moments—those precious instances of joy and connection that, even amidst sorrow, remind us of the beauty in our shared experiences.

This story is not merely about a woman fighting a disease; it is about love that transcends the challenges of illness, the unbreakable bonds between a mother and her children, and the legacy we leave behind. It speaks to the resilience we all possess, the strength found in vulnerability, and the lessons learned in the quiet moments of reflection.

As you turn the pages of this book, I invite you to immerse yourself in the emotional journey of Sarah, John, and Emily. May their story inspire you to embrace life fully, cherish your loved ones, and find hope even in the face of adversity. This is a tale that transcends pain; it is a testament to the indomitable spirit of love, reminding us that every breath we take is a precious gift.

Thank you for joining me on this journey.

ACKNOWLEDGEMENTS

This book is a reflection of the strength, love, and support I've been fortunate to receive.

To my family, who have stood by me through every high and low—your unwavering belief in me gave me the courage to keep going. To my wife and daughter, thank you for your patience and love, even when I was buried in drafts. You are my heart.

To my colleagues and friends, your insights and support have shaped this journey. Thank you for the late-night conversations, the encouragement, and for reminding me of the importance of community.

A special thanks to the healthcare professionals whose dedication inspired many aspects of this story. Your compassion is felt by every patient you touch, and I am grateful for the work you do.

To those living with chronic illness, this book is for you. Your courage, resilience, and hope are the driving force behind these pages. You remind us all that life, even in its hardest moments, can still be full of purpose.

And finally, to my readers: thank you for trusting me with your time. My hope is that this story moves you, challenges you, and leaves you with a sense of connection and hope.

With gratitude,
Mitesh Hood

Prologue

Dr. Sarah Thompson stood at the window of her corner office, gazing out at the sprawling cityscape below. The hospital, with its bustling corridors and incessant hum of activity, was her second home. She had dedicated her life to neurology, driven by a passion to understand the intricacies of the human brain and to help those afflicted by its mysteries. Her patients knew her as a beacon of hope, a doctor who never gave up and always found a way to make them feel heard and cared for.

At forty-two, Sarah had achieved what many only dreamed of. She was the head of the Neurology Department at St. Mary's Hospital, had published numerous groundbreaking research papers, and was often invited to speak at international conferences. Yet, her proudest achievement was her family. Her husband, John, a successful lawyer, was her rock, and their sixteen-year-old daughter, Emily, was the light of her life.

The Thompsons lived in a cozy suburban house, filled with laughter and love. Sarah cherished the evenings spent at home, cooking dinner with John while Emily shared stories about her day at school. They were a tight-knit unit, supporting each other through thick and thin.

But recently, Sarah had noticed something unsettling. It started with a slight drooping of her eyelids, which she attributed to fatigue. After all, balancing a demanding career and a busy family life often left her exhausted. Then, there were the occasional episodes of blurred vision and an inexplicable heaviness in her limbs. She dismissed these as stress-related, convincing herself that a good night's sleep would make it all go away.

One morning, as she was preparing breakfast, she dropped a plate. Her hand simply refused to grip it firmly. John rushed in, concerned, but Sarah brushed it off with a laugh. "Just a bit clumsy today," she said, masking her unease with a smile. Deep down, she knew something was wrong, but the thought of confronting it terrified her. She had always been the one diagnosing and treating others, not the one in need of help.

At work, her colleagues noticed subtle changes. Dr. Michael Roberts, her closest friend and confidant, saw the fatigue in her eyes and the occasional tremor in her hands. "Are you okay, Sarah?" he asked one afternoon, his voice laced with concern.

"I'm fine, Michael. Just a bit tired," she replied, evading his gaze.

But the symptoms persisted. One evening, as she tried to finish a report, her vision blurred to the point where she couldn't read the words on the screen. Panic set in, and she knew she could no longer ignore the signs. Reluctantly, she scheduled an appointment with Dr. Elena Martin, a renowned specialist in autoimmune diseases.

Sitting in Dr. Martin's office, Sarah felt a mix of fear and vulnerability. She had always been the strong one, the doctor with all the answers. Now, she was on the other side, awaiting a diagnosis that could change her life forever.

As Dr. Martin explained the series of tests she would need to undergo, Sarah felt a sense of foreboding. She knew that whatever lay ahead, she would face it head-on, just as she had faced every challenge in her life. Little did she know that this diagnosis would test her resilience and strength in ways she had never imagined.

I

The Diagnosis

Sarah Thompson felt the early morning sun streaming through the window, casting a warm glow over her office. She loved the mornings when the hospital was just waking up, and she could savor a few moments of calm before the day's chaos began. As she sipped her coffee, she noticed her hand trembling slightly. She frowned, setting the cup down. It wasn't the first time she had noticed this unsettling symptom.

For weeks, Sarah had been experiencing a strange heaviness in her limbs and a persistent drooping of her eyelids. At first, she had dismissed it as fatigue, a consequence of her demanding job and the countless hours she dedicated to her patients. But the symptoms were becoming more frequent and more pronounced. Last night, while reading a book to Emily, her vision blurred so badly she had to stop.

"Mom, are you okay?" Emily had asked, her big blue eyes filled with concern.

"I'm fine, sweetheart. Just tired," Sarah had reassured her, forcing a smile. Inside, she was far from reassured.

Today, she had an appointment with Dr. Elena Martin. The thought filled her with dread. Sarah had always been the one diagnosing others, the one providing comfort and solutions. The idea of being a patient herself was terrifying.

As the hours ticked by, Sarah's anxiety grew. She was scheduled to see Dr. Martin at noon, and as the time approached, she found it harder to concentrate. Her mind kept drifting to worst-case scenarios. What if it was something serious? How would she cope?

At eleven-thirty, Sarah left her office and made her way to Dr. Martin's clinic. The walk felt longer than usual, each step weighed down by her fears. She arrived early, her heart pounding in her chest.

"Dr. Thompson, please come in," Dr. Martin's assistant called.

Sarah walked into the office, trying to steady her nerves. Dr. Martin greeted her with a warm smile, but Sarah could see the concern in her eyes.

"Sarah, it's good to see you. How have you been feeling?" Dr. Martin asked as they sat down.

Sarah took a deep breath. "Elena, I've been having some troubling symptoms. Muscle weakness, drooping eyelids, blurred vision... It's been getting worse."

Dr. Martin nodded, listening intently. "We'll run some tests to get to the bottom of this. Don't worry, we'll figure it out."

The tests seemed to drag on forever. Blood work, electromyography, and nerve conduction studies. Sarah felt like she was in a daze, each test chipping away at her facade of calm.

Finally, she sat in Dr. Martin's office again, waiting for the results. The silence was deafening. When Dr. Martin returned, her expression was somber.

"Sarah, the test results are back," she began, her voice gentle. "I'm afraid it's Myasthenia Gravis."

Sarah felt as if the ground had shifted beneath her. "MG? But I'm a neurologist. I know what this means. How can this happen to me?"

Dr. Martin reached out, placing a comforting hand on Sarah's. "I know this is a lot to take in. Myasthenia Gravis is an autoimmune disorder that affects the communication between nerves and muscles. It's rare, but it can be managed with treatment."

Sarah's mind was racing. She knew all about MG – the unpredictable course, the challenges of treatment, the impact on daily life. How was she supposed to balance this with her demanding career and her family?

"I... I need some time to process this," she stammered.

Dr. Martin nodded. "Of course. Take all the time you need. We'll work together to develop a treatment plan that works for you."

Sarah left the clinic in a daze. She walked to her car, her mind swirling with thoughts. How would she tell John and Emily? How would they react? As she sat behind the wheel, tears began to fall. She had always been the strong one, the one in control. Now, she felt powerless.

II

Coping With The News

Sarah left Dr. Martin's office feeling as if she were walking through a fog. The world around her seemed muted, the usual sounds of the bustling hospital fading into a distant hum. She made her way to the parking garage, her mind racing. How was she going to tell John and Emily? How would they react?

As she sat in her car, she stared blankly at the steering wheel, the reality of her diagnosis slowly sinking in. Myasthenia Gravis. The words echoed in her mind, bringing with them a wave of fear and uncertainty. Sarah had always been the strong one, the one in control. Now, she felt powerless, her future shrouded in doubt.

She took a deep breath and started the car, heading home. The drive seemed longer than usual, each mile filled with mounting anxiety. By the time she pulled into the driveway, her hands were trembling again. She sat in the car for a few moments, trying to steady her nerves before going inside.

The familiar sounds of home greeted her as she walked through the door. John was in the kitchen, preparing dinner, and the smell of spaghetti sauce filled the air. Emily was at the dining table, engrossed in her homework. It all seemed so normal, and for a brief second, Sarah wished she could turn back time to a moment before everything changed.

John looked up as she entered. "Hey, honey. You're home early," he said, smiling. But his smile faded as he saw her face. "Sarah, what's wrong?"

Sarah took a deep breath, trying to steady her voice. "John, I need to talk to you. Can we sit down?"

John nodded, wiping his hands on a towel and leading her to the living room. They sat down on the couch, and he took her hands in his. His eyes were filled with concern.

"Sarah, you're scaring me. What's going on?" he asked softly.

Tears welled up in Sarah's eyes as she looked at him. "I went to see Dr. Martin today. I've been having some symptoms... muscle weakness, drooping eyelids, blurred vision. She ran some tests, and... I've been diagnosed with Myasthenia Gravis."

John's face paled. "MG? Oh, Sarah..." He pulled her into a tight embrace, holding her as if he could shield her from the harsh reality of the diagnosis. "We'll get through this together. You're not alone."

Emily walked in, sensing the tension. "Mom, Dad, what's going on?"

Sarah looked at her daughter, her heart breaking. She knew she needed to be strong for Emily. "Emily, come sit with us," she said, patting the spot next to her on the couch.

Emily sat down, her eyes wide with worry. "Mom, what's wrong?"

Sarah took a deep breath, steeling herself. "Emily, I have a condition called Myasthenia Gravis. It's an illness that affects the muscles, making them weak and tired. It's going to be a tough journey, but we'll face it as a family."

Emily's eyes filled with tears. "But Mom, are you going to be okay?"

Sarah wrapped her arms around Emily, holding her close. "We'll get through this together, sweetheart. I promise. It's going to be hard, and there will be challenges, but we'll face them one day at a time."

John put his arm around both of them, forming a tight-knit circle of support. "We're in this together," he said firmly. "We'll do whatever it takes to help you, Sarah."

Later that evening, after Emily had gone to bed, Sarah and John sat together in the living room, trying to process the day's events. The house was quiet, the only sound the ticking of the clock on the mantel.

John broke the silence. "How are you feeling, really?"

Sarah sighed, leaning back against the couch. "I'm scared, John. I know what this disease can do. I've seen patients struggle with it. What if I can't do this? What if I can't be the doctor and the mother I used to be?"

John took her hand, his eyes filled with determination. "Sarah, you are the strongest person I know. You've faced so many challenges in your life, and you've always come out stronger. We will adapt. We'll find new ways to do things. But you don't have to do this alone. We're here for you, every step of the way."

Sarah nodded, tears streaming down her face. "I'm so scared, John."

"I know," he whispered, pulling her close. "But we'll face this together. You are not alone."

The next morning, Sarah decided to share her diagnosis with her colleagues at the hospital. She knew she needed their support, and she wanted to be honest with them about what she was facing. She spent the drive to work rehearsing what she would say, her nerves frayed but her resolve firm.

Gathering everyone in the conference room, she took a deep breath. "I have something important to share with you all," she began. "I've been diagnosed with Myasthenia Gravis, an autoimmune disorder that affects muscle strength. It's going to be a challenging journey, but I want you to know that I'm committed to continuing my work here as much as possible. I will need your support and understanding as I navigate this new reality."

Her colleagues were stunned, but their response was overwhelmingly supportive. Dr. Michael Roberts, her closest friend at the hospital, stood up. "Sarah, we're here for you. We'll do whatever it takes to support you through this. You're not just a colleague; you're family."

The weeks that followed were a whirlwind of doctor's appointments, tests, and treatment plans. Sarah began a regimen of medications to help manage her symptoms, and she worked closely with Dr. Martin to monitor her progress. It wasn't easy. Some days, the fatigue was so overwhelming that she could barely get out of bed. Other days, she felt almost normal, only to be reminded of her illness when her vision blurred or her muscles gave out unexpectedly.

At the hospital, her colleagues rallied around her. They adjusted her schedule to reduce her workload, allowing her more time to rest. They took on extra shifts and responsibilities to ensure that Sarah could focus on her health. The support was overwhelming, and it gave Sarah the strength to keep going.

One evening, as she was tucking Emily into bed, her daughter looked up at her with wide eyes. "Mom, are you going to get better?"

Sarah smiled, brushing a strand of hair from Emily's forehead. "I'm going to do everything I can to manage this illness, Emily. There will be good days and bad days, but I want you to know that no matter what, I will always be here for you."

Emily hugged her tightly. "I love you, Mom."

"I love you too, sweetheart," Sarah whispered, holding her close. "More than anything in the world."

As she left Emily's room, Sarah felt a renewed sense of determination. She knew the road ahead would be filled with challenges, but she was ready to face them. With her family by her side, she believed that anything was possible. She would continue to be the strong, compassionate doctor and mother she had always been, no matter what.

A few weeks later, Sarah sat in her office, reflecting on the journey so far. She had come to realize that Myasthenia Gravis was not just a physical challenge but an emotional and mental one as well. It tested her patience, her resilience, and her ability to adapt. But it also taught her valuable lessons about vulnerability, the importance of support, and the strength of the human spirit.

One afternoon, Dr. Roberts stopped by her office. "How are you holding up?" he asked, leaning against the doorframe.

Sarah looked up and smiled. "It's been tough, but I'm managing. Thanks to all of you."

Dr. Roberts nodded. "We're just doing what we can. You've always been there for us, Sarah. It's only right that we're here for you now."

Sarah felt a lump in her throat. “I can’t thank you enough for everything.”

Dr. Roberts smiled. “You don’t have to. Just keep fighting. We believe in you.”

Sarah nodded, feeling a surge of gratitude. “I will. I promise.”

As the days turned into months, Sarah continued to adapt to her new reality. She learned to listen to her body, to rest when needed, and to ask for help without feeling guilty. She found joy in the small moments, in Emily’s laughter, in quiet evenings with John, and in the camaraderie of her colleagues.

One evening, as the family sat down to dinner, John raised his glass. “To Sarah,” he said, his voice filled with pride. “For her strength, her courage, and her unwavering determination. We’re in this together, and we’re going to get through it, one day at a time.”

Emily raised her glass, smiling. “To Mom.”

Sarah felt tears well up in her eyes as she clinked glasses with her family. “To us,” she said softly. “To love, to strength, and to never giving up.”

As they sat together, sharing stories and laughter, Sarah realized that while Myasthenia Gravis had brought unexpected challenges into her life, it had also brought her closer to her family, her friends, and her own inner strength. She knew the road ahead would not be easy, but with the love and support of those around her, she was ready to face whatever came her way.

III

Beginning The Treatment

Sarah sat in Dr. Martin's office, feeling a mix of apprehension and hope. The room was quiet except for the occasional rustling of papers. Dr. Martin looked up from Sarah's chart, her expression both professional and compassionate.

"We've discussed several treatment options for managing your Myasthenia Gravis," Dr. Martin began. "Given your symptoms and overall health, I recommend starting with a combination of medications, including pyridostigmine to improve communication between your nerves and muscles, and immunosuppressants to reduce your immune system's attack on your body."

Sarah nodded, absorbing the information. "What about side effects?"

Dr. Martin sighed. "There can be side effects, ranging from mild to severe. Nausea, stomach cramps, and increased susceptibility to infections are common. We'll need to monitor you closely, especially in the beginning."

Sarah took a deep breath. "I'm ready to start. I need to do everything I can to manage this disease."

Dr. Martin smiled encouragingly. "That's the spirit, Sarah. Remember, this is a journey, and we'll be with you every step of the way."

The First Steps

Starting treatment was a significant adjustment. The medications left Sarah feeling nauseous and fatigued, but she pushed through, determined to find a balance. She kept a journal to track her symptoms, side effects, and any small improvements. It was her way of taking control, of documenting her fight against the disease.

At home, John and Emily were pillars of support. John took on more household responsibilities, managing the cooking, cleaning, and helping Emily with her homework. Emily, though young, showed remarkable maturity. She would often bring Sarah a glass of water or a blanket, small gestures that meant the world to Sarah.

One evening, as Sarah sat on the couch, her muscles aching and her energy depleted, Emily climbed into her lap with a book. "Mom, can we read together?"

Sarah smiled, feeling a surge of love for her daughter. "Of course, sweetheart. What book do you have?"

Emily held up her favorite storybook, and together they read, Sarah's voice steady despite the fatigue. Moments like these reminded Sarah why she was fighting so hard. She was determined to be there for Emily, to share in her life's moments, big and small.

Support from Colleagues

At the hospital, Sarah received unwavering support from her colleagues. They reshaped her schedule, lightening her workload to give her the rest she needed. Dr. Roberts, in particular, made it a point to check in regularly, offering not only medical guidance but also a steady presence of personal encouragement.

One morning, Sarah walked into the staff lounge to find a group of her colleagues gathered. Dr. Roberts stepped forward with a smile. "Sarah, we've been talking, and we wanted to do something to show our support. We've started a rotating schedule to cover your shifts when you need rest, and we've also arranged for a counselor to be available for you anytime you need to talk."

Sarah felt tears prick her eyes. "Thank you all so much. I don't know what I would do without your support."

Dr. Roberts hugged her gently. "We're a family here, Sarah. We take care of our own."

The emotional support from her colleagues was invaluable. Knowing that she had a team of people who cared about her well-being gave Sarah the strength to push through the tough days. She felt a renewed sense of purpose, both as a doctor and as a patient navigating her own health challenges.

Emotional and Physical Struggles

Despite the support and her determination, the journey was far from easy. There were days when the fatigue was so overwhelming that Sarah could barely get out of bed. Her muscles would weaken without warning, making even the simplest tasks difficult.

One particularly challenging day, Sarah found herself struggling to hold a cup of coffee. Her hands trembled, and the cup slipped, shattering on the floor. The frustration and helplessness were overwhelming, and she sank to the floor in tears.

John rushed to her side, kneeling beside her and wrapping her in his arms. "It's okay, Sarah. It's okay. We'll get through this."

Sarah sobbed into his shoulder. "I feel so weak, John. I hate this. I hate feeling like I can't do anything."

John held her tightly, his own eyes filled with unshed tears. "You are not weak, Sarah. You are one of the strongest people I know. It's okay to feel frustrated. It's okay to cry. We'll face this together."

Sarah clung to him, drawing strength from his unwavering support. Slowly, her sobs subsided, replaced by a determination to keep fighting. She knew the road ahead would be difficult, but she also knew she wasn't alone.

Finding Strength in Community

As Sarah's condition progressed, the weight of her diagnosis became harder to bear in isolation. Despite John's constant support and Emily's growing understanding, there were moments when the medical professional in her craved to connect with others who truly understood the daily battle of living with myasthenia gravis. She realized that while her family stood beside her, they couldn't fully grasp the physical and emotional toll that the disease exacted.

One evening, after a particularly tough day of treatment, Sarah sat in her office, feeling the loneliness of her journey. She reflected on the countless patients she had treated, how many of them had found healing not just through medical care but also through shared experiences with others facing similar struggles. It was then that an idea sparked within her—a support group.

She envisioned a space where people like her could gather, share their stories, and lean on one another during the darkest moments. Sarah had spent her career guiding others through their battles; now it was time to create a community that could uplift one another.

The very next day, she approached the hospital administration with her plan. "I want to create a support group for people living with chronic illnesses," she explained passionately. "I know firsthand how isolating it can feel, and sometimes, just knowing someone else understands can be as healing as any treatment."

The hospital administration agreed wholeheartedly, offering her a room to host the meetings. Sarah began spreading the word, reaching out to patients, colleagues, and even those she encountered online in the myasthenia gravis community. It didn't take long for the group to form.

At the first meeting, Sarah walked into a room filled with faces that mirrored her own sense of exhaustion, fear, and hope. As they sat in a circle, she felt a surge of nervousness—she was no longer the doctor in this room; she was one of them.

"I'm Sarah," she said, her voice trembling slightly. "I've spent my life helping others navigate their illnesses, but now I'm in the same boat as all of you. I was diagnosed with myasthenia gravis, and it's been... it's been hard. But I'm hoping that together, we can find strength in each other."

The room fell silent for a moment before one woman, who had been quietly observing, spoke up. "I've been living with this for five years," she said. "And I thought I was the only one who felt this way."

Another man nodded in agreement, his voice raw with emotion. "The hardest part isn't even the illness itself. It's the isolation, feeling like no one around you really gets what you're going through."

In that moment, Sarah realized she had made the right decision. This group wasn't just for her—it was for all of them. As the weeks went by, the support group grew into something much bigger than she had anticipated. Each meeting became a lifeline for the members, where they could share their frustrations, victories, and everything in between.

Sarah found that the simple act of listening and sharing stories lightened her burden. Every person in the room had their own fight, their own version of pain and triumph, but together, they built something stronger than the disease. They exchanged tips on how to manage symptoms, shared experiences with medications, and most importantly, they offered each other understanding.

Though her physical strength often wavered, the emotional strength she drew from the group gave her a renewed sense of purpose. In creating this community, Sarah found herself healing in ways that medicine alone could not provide. The support group meetings became a beacon of hope, reminding her that even in the hardest moments, she was never truly alone.

In giving others a space to share their struggles, Sarah found a deeper connection to herself, realizing that her strength didn't come from facing the disease alone, but in allowing herself to lean on others when she needed it most. The support group was more than just a meeting—it was a community of warriors, and Sarah was proud to stand alongside them.

A Family United

At home, Sarah and her family continued to adapt to their new normal. John's support was unwavering, and Emily's maturity and kindness were a constant source of comfort. They found new ways to spend time together, cherishing the small moments that brought joy and connection.

One weekend, they decided to take a trip to a nearby park. It was a beautiful autumn day, the air crisp and the leaves a vibrant tapestry of reds and yellows. They packed a picnic and set out, determined to enjoy the day together.

As they walked along the park's winding paths, Sarah felt a sense of peace. The fresh air and the beauty of nature were a balm for her weary soul. They found a quiet spot by a lake and spread out their picnic blanket, sharing a simple meal and enjoying each other's company.

Emily ran ahead, her laughter echoing through the trees as she chased a squirrel. Sarah watched her, a smile tugging at her lips. "She's so full of life," she said softly.

John took her hand, squeezing it gently. "She gets that from you, you know. Your strength, your resilience. She sees it every day."

Sarah leaned her head on his shoulder. "I hope so. I want her to know that no matter what life throws at us, we can always find a way through."

John kissed her forehead. "We will, Sarah. Together, we can face anything."

Looking Forward

As the months passed, Sarah continued to navigate the challenges of living with Myasthenia Gravis. There were good days and bad days, but she learned to cherish the good moments and find strength in the difficult ones. She remained dedicated to her work, her family, and the support group, finding purpose and fulfilment in each role.

One evening, as she sat at her desk, she received an email from a patient in the support group. The patient, a young woman named Lisa, wrote about how much the group had helped her, how Sarah's strength and vulnerability had inspired her to keep fighting.

Sarah read the email with tears in her eyes, feeling a profound sense of gratitude. She realized that despite the challenges, she was making a difference. She was helping others find hope and strength, just as she had found her own.

As she closed her laptop and headed to bed, Sarah felt a deep sense of peace. She knew that the road ahead would continue to be challenging, but she also knew that she had the love and support of her family, friends, and colleagues. She was not alone, and that made all the difference.

Lying in bed, she listened to the gentle rhythm of John's breathing beside her, the comforting sounds of home. She closed her eyes, a smile on her lips, ready to face whatever tomorrow would bring. For Sarah, the journey was about more than just managing a disease; it was about embracing life, finding joy in the small moments, and never giving up hope. And with the love and support of those around her, she knew she could face anything.

IV

Life Adjustments

Sarah sat at her desk, staring at her calendar. Adjusting her work schedule felt like admitting defeat, but she knew it was necessary. The fatigue and muscle weakness were becoming more unpredictable, and she needed to find a balance between her health and her responsibilities as a doctor.

Dr. Roberts had been incredibly supportive. "We'll make this work, Sarah," he had reassured her. "You're a valuable member of this team, and we need you to be at your best. Let's find a way to keep you involved without overburdening you."

They decided to shift some of her more physically demanding duties to other colleagues and increase her focus on administrative tasks, mentoring, and research. It wasn't the same as being on the front lines with her patients, but it was important work nonetheless.

The Impact on Professional Life

The changes in Sarah's role at the hospital were both a relief and a source of deep frustration. She missed the direct patient care that had driven her passion for medicine. The energy of the emergency room, the satisfaction of a successful surgery, the joy of seeing patients recover—these were the moments that had defined her career. Now, she found herself spending more time behind a desk, pouring over research papers and administrative forms.

One afternoon, Sarah was reviewing patient charts when a knock on her door interrupted her thoughts. It was Dr. Emily Collins, a younger colleague who had always looked up to Sarah.

"Dr. Thompson, I was wondering if I could get your advice on a case," Emily said, stepping into the office.

"Of course, Emily. What's going on?" Sarah replied, grateful for the distraction.

Emily explained a complex case involving a young patient with an unusual set of symptoms. As Sarah listened and offered her insights, she felt a familiar spark of excitement. Even though she wasn't the one diagnosing the patient firsthand, she realized she could still contribute significantly to her colleagues' work.

"Thank you, Dr. Thompson. Your perspective is always so valuable," Emily said with a smile.

Sarah returned the smile, feeling a sense of pride and purpose. "Anytime, Emily. Remember, we're all in this together."

Finding New Ways to Contribute

Sarah began to embrace her new role with a renewed sense of purpose. She started hosting regular mentoring sessions for younger doctors, sharing her experiences and guiding them through challenging cases. Her knowledge and expertise became a vital resource for the hospital staff.

In addition to mentoring, Sarah delved deeper into medical research. She collaborated with a team of researchers studying Myasthenia Gravis, hoping to contribute to advancements in understanding and treating the disease. The work was demanding but deeply fulfilling. It gave her a sense of control over her condition, as if she were fighting back against it by helping to unlock its secrets.

One evening, as Sarah was engrossed in a research paper, John walked into the room with two cups of tea. He set one down beside her and sat across from her.

"You've been working so hard lately," he said, concern in his voice. "How are you feeling?"

Sarah took a sip of tea, feeling the warmth spread through her. "I'm tired, but it's a good kind of tired. The research is really engaging, and mentoring the younger doctors gives me a sense of purpose. It's different from what I'm used to, but it's meaningful."

John reached across the table and took her hand. "I'm glad to hear that. Just promise me you'll take care of yourself too. We need you, Sarah."

Sarah squeezed his hand, a lump forming in her throat. "I promise, John. Thank you for always being there for me."

Personal Life Adjustments

At home, the adjustments were just as significant. Sarah had always been the backbone of the household, managing everything from Emily's school activities to the household chores. Now, she had to learn to rely on John and Emily more, a shift that was both humbling and heartwarming.

One Saturday morning, Sarah was sitting at the kitchen table, reviewing some research notes, when Emily bounded into the room.

"Mom, can we bake cookies today?" Emily asked, her eyes sparkling with excitement.

Sarah hesitated, thinking about the physical effort involved. But before she could respond, John walked in, a smile on his face. "How about I handle the heavy lifting, and you two handle the fun part?"

Emily's face lit up. "Yes! Let's do it!"

Sarah smiled, feeling a wave of gratitude. "Alright, let's make some cookies."

As they worked together in the kitchen, Sarah felt a sense of normalcy returning. She mixed the ingredients while John handled the oven and heavy lifting, and Emily delighted in decorating the cookies. It was a simple activity, but it was filled with laughter and love.

Later, as they sat together enjoying the freshly baked cookies, Emily looked up at her mother. "Mom, I'm glad we can still do fun things together."

Sarah felt a lump in her throat and pulled Emily into a hug. "Me too, sweetheart. Me too."

Community Support

The support group Sarah had started at the hospital also became a crucial part of her life. Each meeting was a reminder of the strength and resilience that could be found in shared experiences. The group members had become like an extended family, each story and struggle forging deeper bonds.

During one particularly moving session, a new member, James, shared his story. He was a retired firefighter who had been diagnosed with Parkinson's disease. As he spoke about the challenges of losing his physical abilities and the emotional toll it had taken, the group listened with empathy and understanding.

Sarah felt a profound connection to James's story. When it was her turn to speak, she shared her own journey, the highs and lows, and the ways she had learned to adapt.

"Living with a chronic illness changes your life in ways you never imagined," Sarah said, her voice steady but filled with emotion. "But it also teaches you about strength, resilience, and the importance of leaning on others. We're not alone in this journey, and that makes all the difference."

James nodded, tears in his eyes. "Thank you, Sarah. It means a lot to hear that."

After the meeting, James approached Sarah. "I've been feeling so isolated, like no one understands what I'm going through. This group, and hearing your story, it's given me hope."

Sarah smiled, feeling a sense of fulfillment. "We're all here for each other, James. You're not alone."

A New Perspective

As Sarah continued to navigate her new normal, she found herself reflecting on the journey so far. The initial shock and fear had given way to acceptance and adaptation. She had learned to cherish the small moments, to find joy in the everyday, and to draw strength from the people around her.

One evening, as Sarah sat on the porch with John, watching the sun set, she felt a sense of peace. The sky was painted in hues of orange and pink, a beautiful reminder of the world's endless possibilities.

"Do you ever think about what life would be like if things were different?" Sarah asked, her voice soft.

John looked at her, his eyes filled with love. "Sometimes. But then I remember that we can't change the past. We can only move forward and make the best of what we have."

Sarah nodded, feeling the truth of his words. "You're right. And I'm grateful for every moment we have together. This journey has been hard, but it's also shown me how much love and support we have."

John took her hand, squeezing it gently. "We're stronger together, Sarah. No matter what comes our way, we'll face it together."

Sarah leaned her head on his shoulder, feeling a deep sense of contentment. She knew there would be more challenges ahead, but she also knew she was not alone. With the love of her family, the support of her colleagues, and the strength of her community, she felt ready to face whatever the future held.

As the stars began to twinkle in the night sky, Sarah closed her eyes and took a deep breath. Life with Myasthenia Gravis was a constant adjustment, but it was also a journey filled with love, resilience, and hope. And for Sarah, that was enough.

V

Finding Strength

The days were growing shorter as autumn settled in, the leaves turning brilliant shades of red and gold. Sarah found herself reflecting on the changes in her life, both the ones that had been forced upon her and those she had chosen to embrace. She was learning to find strength in unexpected places, to adapt and grow despite the challenges she faced.

Unexpected Moments of Strength

One crisp morning, Sarah stood in front of the mirror, taking in her reflection. She noticed the faint lines around her eyes, the subtle signs of the battles she had been fighting. She had lost some weight due to the medications, and her skin seemed paler, but her eyes still held the spark of determination.

"Ready for another day, Sarah?" she whispered to herself, a small smile playing on her lips.

As she got dressed, she felt a new kind of strength within her, one that came not from physical prowess but from the resilience of her spirit. She had learned to adapt, to find ways to continue living her life to the fullest despite the limitations imposed by her condition.

At the hospital, her colleagues had started to see her as a symbol of perseverance. Dr. Emily Collins often came to her for advice, and the younger doctors looked up to her not just for her medical expertise, but for her strength in the face of adversity.

A Patient's Story

One day, Sarah was asked to consult on a particularly challenging case. A young woman named Mia had been admitted with severe respiratory issues. The initial tests were inconclusive, and the doctors were struggling to diagnose her condition. Sarah was known for her keen diagnostic skills, and Dr. Roberts had specifically requested her input.

"Mia's case is complicated," Dr. Roberts explained as they reviewed the charts. "She's been through multiple tests, but we still don't have a clear diagnosis."

Sarah studied the charts, noting the various symptoms and test results. She felt a familiar sense of purpose, the thrill of a medical mystery waiting to be solved. As she delved deeper into Mia's history, something clicked.

"I think we might be looking at an autoimmune condition," Sarah said thoughtfully. "Her symptoms could be indicative of a rare form of lupus."

Dr. Roberts nodded, considering her suggestion. "It's definitely a possibility. Let's run the appropriate tests and see if we can confirm it."

The tests confirmed Sarah's suspicion, and Mia was started on a treatment plan. Over the next few weeks, Sarah visited Mia regularly, checking on her progress and offering support.

"You've been through a lot," Sarah said one afternoon, sitting by Mia's bedside. "But you're strong, and we're going to get through this together."

Mia looked at Sarah, her eyes filled with gratitude. "Thank you, Dr. Thompson. Your faith in me means a lot."

Sarah smiled, feeling a sense of fulfillment. Moments like these reminded her why she had chosen this path, why she continued to fight despite her own struggles.

Personal Growth and Epiphanies

As the weeks passed, Sarah found herself growing in unexpected ways. She had always been focused on her career, driven by a desire to help others. Now, she was learning to help herself as well, to find balance and peace in her own life.

One evening, Sarah sat on the porch with a cup of tea, watching the sun set. John joined her, sitting close and taking her hand in his.

"You've been quiet today," John said gently. "What's on your mind?"

Sarah sighed, leaning her head on his shoulder. "I've been thinking about everything that's happened, about how much has changed. I feel like I've been forced to slow down, to really look at my life."

John nodded, his thumb rubbing soothing circles on her hand. "And what do you see?"

Sarah smiled softly. "I see a woman who's learned to find strength in vulnerability, who's discovered that it's okay to lean on others. I've always been so focused on being strong for everyone else, but I've realized that it's just as important to be strong for myself."

John kissed her temple, his love for her evident in his eyes. "You've always been strong, Sarah. But I think you're right. It's about finding balance, about allowing yourself to be human."

Sarah nodded, feeling a sense of peace settle over her. She knew the road ahead would continue to be challenging, but she also knew she had the strength to face it, not just for herself, but for her family and her patients.

Inspirational Interactions with Patients

Sarah's newfound strength and perspective began to influence her interactions with her patients. She found herself connecting with them on a deeper level, understanding their fears and hopes in a way she hadn't before.

One patient, an elderly man named Henry, had been battling cancer for years. He was nearing the end of his journey, and Sarah had been asked to provide palliative care. She visited him regularly, sitting by his bedside and listening to his stories.

"Life is funny," Henry said one afternoon, his voice weak but steady. "You spend so much time worrying about the future, and then you realize it's the little moments that matter the most."

Sarah nodded, feeling the truth of his words. "It's those moments that give life its meaning, isn't it?"

Henry smiled, a twinkle in his eye. "Exactly. I've had a good life, Dr. Thompson. I've loved and been loved. And now, I'm ready for whatever comes next."

Sarah felt a lump in her throat, moved by Henry's acceptance and peace. "You've been incredibly brave, Henry. It's an honor to be here with you."

Henry squeezed her hand, his grip surprisingly strong. "Thank you, Dr. Thompson. You've made this journey a little easier."

As she left Henry's room, Sarah felt a deep sense of gratitude. Her patients taught her as much as she taught them, each interaction a reminder of the resilience of the human spirit.

Strength in Vulnerability

Sarah's journey was not without its setbacks. There were days when her body betrayed her, when the fatigue and muscle weakness were overwhelming. On those days, she leaned on John and Emily, drawing strength from their unwavering support.

One particularly difficult evening, Sarah was sitting on the couch, feeling exhausted and frustrated. Emily climbed into her lap, wrapping her small arms around her mother.

"It's okay, Mom," Emily whispered. "You're the strongest person I know."

Sarah felt tears prick her eyes, moved by her daughter's words. She hugged Emily tightly, feeling a surge of love and determination. "Thank you, sweetheart. You make me stronger every day."

John joined them, sitting beside Sarah and pulling her into his embrace. "We're a team, remember? We'll get through this together."

Sarah leaned into John, feeling a sense of comfort and safety. She knew that no matter what challenges lay ahead, she had the love and support of her family to guide her.

Looking Forward

As autumn gave way to winter, Sarah continued to find strength in the small moments, in the connections she forged with her patients and the love of her family. She knew the road ahead would be filled with ups and downs, but she was ready to face it with courage and resilience.

One evening, as snow began to fall outside, Sarah sat by the fire with John and Emily. They were decorating the Christmas tree, each ornament a reminder of the memories they had created together.

"This is my favorite time of year," Emily said, hanging a sparkling star on the tree. "It's so magical."

Sarah smiled, feeling the warmth of the fire and the love of her family. "It is magical, Emily. It's a time to celebrate the things that matter most."

John wrapped an arm around Sarah, pulling her close. "And what matters most is us, together."

Sarah nodded, feeling a deep sense of peace. "Yes, together."

As they sat by the fire, watching the snow fall outside, Sarah felt a renewed sense of hope and strength. She knew there would be challenges ahead, but she also knew she had the love and support of her family and friends to guide her. And for Sarah, that was enough.

VI

Emily's Struggles

The autumn breeze rustled through the trees, sending a cascade of golden leaves to the ground as Emily walked home from school. Her steps were heavy, and her mind was weighed down by thoughts of her mother. The other kids didn't understand what it was like to have a parent with a chronic illness, and it often made Emily feel isolated.

At school, the whispers and stares from her classmates were becoming more frequent. They didn't mean to be cruel, but their curiosity and lack of understanding about Sarah's condition created an invisible barrier. Emily had always been a bright and outgoing student, but lately, she felt herself withdrawing.

One afternoon, during a group project, Emily's friend Lily turned to her with a hesitant look. "Emily, are you okay? You've seemed really quiet lately."

Emily forced a smile. "I'm fine, Lily. Just tired, I guess."

Lily frowned, clearly not convinced. "You know you can talk to me, right? If something's bothering you..."

Emily nodded, appreciating the sentiment but not wanting to burden her friend with the complexities of her home life. “Thanks, Lily. I’ll be okay.”

A Difficult Day

That evening, as Emily walked through the front door, she heard the familiar sound of her mother’s voice. Sarah was sitting at the kitchen table, a stack of medical journals in front of her. She looked up and smiled as Emily entered.

“Hey, sweetheart. How was school?” Sarah asked, her eyes filled with warmth.

Emily shrugged, dropping her backpack by the door. “It was fine.”

Sarah could sense the underlying tension in her daughter’s voice. “Do you want to talk about it?”

Emily shook her head, heading for the stairs. “Not really. I have homework to do.”

Sarah watched her daughter retreat to her room, her heart aching with the knowledge that Emily was struggling. She knew that her illness had affected Emily deeply, and she wished she could shield her from the pain and uncertainty.

The Heart-to-Heart

Later that evening, as the house grew quiet, Sarah knocked softly on Emily’s door. “Can I come in?”

Emily was sitting at her desk, staring blankly at her homework. She nodded, not looking up. “Sure, Mom.”

Sarah entered and sat on the edge of the bed, her eyes gentle and concerned. “Emily, I can tell something’s been bothering you. You don’t have to keep it all inside. I’m here for you.”

Emily’s eyes filled with tears, and she turned to face her mother. “It’s just... it’s hard, Mom. Everyone at school keeps asking questions, and I don’t know what to say. I don’t want them to pity me or think I’m different.”

Sarah reached out and took Emily’s hand, squeezing it gently. “I know it’s difficult, sweetheart. It’s okay to feel upset and overwhelmed. You're going through a lot."

Emily sniffled, wiping her eyes with the back of her hand. "I just wish things could go back to the way they were before you got sick. I hate seeing you struggle."

Sarah felt a lump in her throat, tears welling up in her own eyes. "I know, Emily. I wish I could make it all better, but we have to face this together. You're not alone in this. We're a team, remember?"

Emily nodded, her voice trembling. "I just don't know how to be strong all the time. Sometimes it feels like too much."

Sarah pulled her daughter into a hug, holding her tightly. "You don't have to be strong all the time, Emily. It's okay to feel scared and sad. We'll get through this together, one step at a time."

The Teasing Incident

The following week, Emily was sitting alone at lunch when a group of girls approached her table. They were led by Madison, a girl who had always been a bit of a bully.

"Hey, Emily," Madison said with a smirk. "We heard your mom's really sick. Is she going to die or something?"

Emily felt her face flush with anger and embarrassment. "No, she's not going to die. She has a chronic illness, but she's managing it."

Madison's friends giggled, and Madison continued to press. "But isn't she like, really weak all the time? My mom said people with that kind of disease can't even walk properly."

Emily clenched her fists under the table, trying to keep her composure. "She has good days and bad days, but she's strong. Stronger than you'll ever know."

One of the other girls, Jessica, chimed in with a mocking tone. "Do you have to take care of her all the time? That must be so annoying."

Tears prickled at the corners of Emily's eyes, but she refused to let them fall. "It's not annoying. She's my mom, and I love her. You wouldn't understand."

Madison rolled her eyes. "Whatever, Emily. Just don't expect us to feel sorry for you."

The girls walked away, leaving Emily feeling humiliated and alone. She picked at her lunch, her appetite gone, and tried to hold back the sobs threatening to escape.

Finding Support

That evening, Sarah decided to talk to Emily's teacher, Mrs. Johnson, about what Emily was going through. She wanted to make sure Emily had the support she needed at school.

"Thank you for meeting with me, Mrs. Johnson," Sarah said as they sat in the teacher's office. "Emily has been having a hard time lately, and I think she could use some extra support."

Mrs. Johnson nodded, her expression sympathetic. "I've noticed that Emily has seemed more withdrawn recently. I'm glad you came to talk to me about it. We'll do everything we can to support her."

Sarah felt a sense of relief. "Thank you. It means a lot to know she's not alone in this."

Mrs. Johnson smiled warmly. "Emily is a wonderful student. We'll make sure she has the support she needs."

That evening, Sarah and John sat down with Emily to talk about the meeting with her teacher.

"Mrs. Johnson was very understanding," Sarah said. "She wants to make sure you have the support you need at school."

Emily looked up, a mixture of relief and anxiety in her eyes. "What does that mean?"

"It means that if you ever need to talk, or if you're having a tough day, you can go to her," John explained. "She's there to help you, Emily. You don't have to go through this alone."

Emily nodded slowly, taking in their words. "Okay. Thanks, Mom. Thanks, Dad."

A New Friend

A few days later, during lunch, Emily was sitting alone when a girl from her science class, Sophie, approached her.

"Hey, Emily. Mind if I sit here?" Sophie asked, holding her lunch tray.

Emily looked up, surprised but grateful for the company. "Sure, go ahead."

Sophie sat down, giving Emily a friendly smile. "I heard about your mom. My dad has been sick for a while too, so I kind of understand what you're going through."

Emily's eyes widened. "Really? What's wrong with him?"

Sophie sighed, her expression somber. "He has multiple sclerosis. It's been really hard on our family, but we've learned to manage."

Emily felt a connection with Sophie, a sense of relief that someone understood. "It's hard to explain to other kids, you know? They just don't get it."

Sophie nodded. "Yeah, I know. But you're not alone. If you ever need someone to talk to, I'm here."

Emily smiled, feeling a weight lift off her shoulders. "Thanks, Sophie. I'd like that."

Strength in Community

Over the next few weeks, Emily and Sophie became close friends, sharing their experiences and supporting each other. Emily felt less isolated, knowing she had someone who understood what she was going through.

At home, Emily continued to open up to her parents, and they found ways to cope together. They started having regular family meetings to talk about their feelings and support each other.

One evening, as they sat around the dinner table, Emily looked at her parents and felt a surge of gratitude. "I'm glad we're in this together," she said, her voice filled with emotion.

Sarah reached across the table and took Emily's hand. "Me too, sweetheart. We're stronger together."

John nodded, his eyes shining with pride. "No matter what, we'll always have each other."

Moving Forward

As winter approached, Emily found herself feeling more hopeful. She still had difficult days, but she knew she had a strong support system both at home and at school.

One cold December morning, Sarah and Emily were sitting on the porch, wrapped in blankets and sipping hot cocoa. The snow was falling gently, covering the ground in a pristine white blanket.

"It's beautiful, isn't it?" Sarah said, her breath visible in the cold air.

Emily nodded, her eyes fixed on the falling snow. "Yeah, it is. It feels peaceful."

Sarah smiled, feeling a sense of contentment. "I think this winter is going to be different, Emily. We've learned so much about each other, and about ourselves. We're stronger now."

Emily leaned her head on her mother's shoulder, feeling the warmth of their bond. "I think you're right, Mom. We are stronger."

As they sat together, watching the snow fall, Sarah felt a renewed sense of hope for the future. She knew there would still be challenges ahead, but she also knew that, together, they could face anything.

A Message of Hope

In the following months, Emily began to thrive. With the support of her family, friends, and teachers, she found new ways to cope with the challenges of her mother's illness. She became more confident, more resilient, and more compassionate.

Sarah watched with pride as her daughter blossomed, knowing that their journey had made them both stronger. She continued to find strength in her family and in the small moments of joy that life offered.

One evening, as they sat together by the fire, Emily turned to her mother with a thoughtful expression. "Mom, do you think things will ever go back to the way they were before?"

Sarah smiled, brushing a strand of hair from Emily's face. "Things may never be exactly the same, but that's okay. We've learned to adapt, to find strength in each other. And in some ways, I think we're better for it."

Emily nodded, a sense of peace settling over her. "I think you're right, Mom. We're stronger together."

As they sat by the fire, the warmth of their love and support enveloping them, Sarah knew that they would face whatever challenges lay ahead with courage and resilience. They were a team, and together, they could conquer anything.

The snow continued to fall outside, a beautiful reminder of the world's endless possibilities. And for Sarah and Emily, the future was filled with hope and strength, a testament to the unbreakable bond they shared.

VII

John's Support

John Parker had always been a man of few words, preferring to express his love through actions rather than lengthy declarations. When he first met Sarah, he was drawn to her passion for life and her unwavering dedication to her work as a doctor. Over the years, their bond had only grown stronger, built on a foundation of mutual respect and shared dreams.

But Sarah's diagnosis of myasthenia gravis had thrown their lives into turmoil. John found himself navigating a new reality, where the woman he loved was often tired and in pain. He watched helplessly as the disease stole pieces of her strength, leaving her vulnerable and frustrated. Despite the challenges, John was determined to be the rock Sarah needed, to support her through every trial and triumph.

A Daily Routine

The sound of the alarm clock jolted John awake at 5:30 a.m., as it did every morning. He reached over to turn it off before it could wake Sarah, who was still sleeping soundly beside him. Her face, illuminated by the soft morning light, looked peaceful. John smiled gently, leaning over to plant a kiss on her forehead.

He slipped out of bed quietly and headed to the kitchen to start the coffee. The aroma filled the house, a familiar comfort. As he prepared breakfast, John's mind wandered to the day ahead. He had a full schedule at the construction site, but his thoughts were never far from Sarah and Emily.

When Sarah joined him in the kitchen, John could see the fatigue in her eyes. "Good morning, beautiful," he greeted her with a warm smile. "How are you feeling today?"

Sarah managed a tired smile in return. "Morning, John. I'm okay. Just a bit more tired than usual."

John reached out and took her hand. "Take it easy today, alright? I'll handle dinner tonight. How about your favorite pasta?"

Sarah's eyes sparkled with gratitude. "That sounds wonderful. Thank you, John."

John squeezed her hand gently. "Anything for you, love."

Navigating Strains

Despite their unwavering love, the strain of Sarah's illness began to take its toll on their marriage. The emotional and physical demands of her condition were immense, and there were days when John felt overwhelmed by the weight of it all. The once spontaneous and adventurous couple now found themselves confined to a routine dictated by Sarah's health.

One evening, after a particularly challenging day at work, John returned home to find Sarah struggling to open a jar of pickles for dinner. The simple task seemed monumental in her weakened state. John's heart ached at the sight, but his exhaustion got the better of him.

"Why didn't you wait for me?" he asked, his tone sharper than he intended. "I could have helped."

Sarah's eyes filled with tears. "I wanted to do something myself for a change. I hate feeling so helpless."

John immediately regretted his harsh words. He took the jar from her hands and set it aside, pulling her into a gentle embrace. "I'm sorry, Sarah. I didn't mean to snap at you. It's just... hard sometimes, you know?"

Sarah nodded against his chest, her tears dampening his shirt. "I know, John. It's hard for me too. But we're in this together, right?"

John kissed the top of her head. "Always. We'll get through this, one day at a time."

Reaffirming Their Love

Despite the challenges, there were moments that reaffirmed their love and commitment to each other. One such moment came on a quiet Sunday afternoon. Emily was out with friends, and the house was unusually still. John suggested they watch a movie, something light-hearted to lift their spirits.

As they settled on the couch, Sarah snuggled into John's side, her head resting on his shoulder. The movie played in the background, but their focus was on each other. John looked down at Sarah, marveling at her resilience and strength.

"Do you remember our first date?" John asked softly, a smile playing on his lips.

Sarah looked up at him, her eyes shining with nostalgia. "Of course I do. You took me to that little Italian restaurant downtown. We talked for hours."

John chuckled. "And we ended up missing the last bus home. We had to walk for miles, but it was worth it."

Sarah's laughter was like music to his ears. "It was. I knew then that you were someone special."

John's expression grew serious. "Sarah, I know things are tough right now, but I want you to know that I'm here for you. I love you more than anything, and we'll get through this together."

Sarah's eyes filled with tears, but this time they were tears of gratitude and love. "I love you too, John. Thank you for being my rock."

They leaned in and shared a tender kiss, a reaffirmation of their love and commitment. In that moment, all the struggles and hardships seemed to fade away, leaving only the deep bond they shared.

Emily's Struggles and Triumphs

The following Monday, Emily walked into her classroom with a sense of trepidation. The teasing incident was still fresh in her mind, and she dreaded facing her classmates. As she took her seat, she noticed Madison and her friends whispering and glancing in her direction.

During lunch, Emily sat alone, picking at her food. She heard footsteps approaching and braced herself for more taunts. To her surprise, it was Sophie who sat down beside her.

"Hey, Emily," Sophie said with a warm smile. "Mind if I join you?"

Emily looked up, relieved. "Not at all. Thanks, Sophie."

Sophie glanced at Madison's table and then back at Emily. "I heard what happened last week. Madison can be really mean sometimes. Don't let her get to you."

Emily sighed. "It's hard. They don't understand what it's like."

Sophie nodded empathetically. "I know. But you're not alone. My dad's illness has taught me that it's okay to feel sad and overwhelmed. We just have to take it one day at a time."

Emily felt a weight lift off her shoulders. "Thanks, Sophie. It helps to talk to someone who understands."

As the weeks passed, Emily and Sophie became close friends. Emily found solace in their conversations and began to open up more at home. She told her parents about the teasing incident, and they reassured her that she was strong and brave.

John's Perspective

John's support for Sarah extended beyond their home. He often found himself researching myasthenia gravis, looking for new treatments and ways to make Sarah's life easier. One evening, after Emily had gone to bed, John shared his findings with Sarah.

"I found a support group for families dealing with myasthenia gravis," John said, showing Sarah the website. "I think it could be helpful for both of us."

Sarah looked at the screen, then back at John. "You're amazing, you know that? Thank you for always looking out for us."

John smiled, taking her hand in his. "We're in this together, remember? I'll do whatever it takes to make sure you're okay."

Sarah leaned in and kissed him. "I'm so grateful for you, John. I don't know what I'd do without you."

John's eyes softened with love. "You'll never have to find out, Sarah. I'm not going anywhere."

Facing Challenges Together

Despite the strain on their marriage, John and Sarah found strength in their shared love and commitment. They attended the support group meetings together, finding comfort in the stories and experiences of others facing similar challenges. The group became a source of strength, a reminder that they were not alone.

One evening, after a particularly uplifting support group meeting, John and Sarah sat on the porch, watching the stars.

"Tonight was really helpful," Sarah said, her voice filled with hope. "Hearing other people's stories makes me feel less alone."

John nodded, his arm wrapped around her shoulders. "It does. We're all in this together, and we're stronger for it."

Sarah rested her head on his shoulder, feeling a sense of peace. "Thank you, John. For everything."

John kissed the top of her head. "You don't have to thank me, Sarah. I love you, and I always will."

As they sat together under the starry sky, John felt a renewed sense of determination. No matter what challenges lay ahead, he knew they would face them together, hand in hand. Their love was a beacon of light, guiding them through the darkest of times.

A New Normal

With time, the Parker family found a new rhythm. They adjusted to the ups and downs of Sarah's condition, finding joy in the small moments and strength in each other. Emily continued to thrive with the support of her family and friends, and John remained a steadfast pillar of strength for Sarah.

One sunny afternoon, as they sat in the backyard, Emily turned to her parents with a thoughtful expression. "Do you think things will ever be the same again?"

John exchanged a look with Sarah before answering. "Things may never be exactly the same, Emily. But that's okay. We've learned to adapt, to find strength in each other. And in some ways, we're better for it."

Sarah nodded, her eyes filled with love. "We're stronger together, Emily. And we always will be."

Emily smiled, feeling a sense of peace. “I think you’re right. We are stronger.”

As they sat together, basking in the warmth of the afternoon sun, John felt a deep sense of gratitude. Despite the challenges they had faced, they had come through stronger and more united than ever. Their love and commitment to each other were unbreakable, a testament to the power of resilience and hope.

The future was uncertain, but John knew that as long as they had each other, they could face anything. Together, they were unstoppable.

VIII

A New Purpose

Sarah's diagnosis had been life-altering, but as time passed, she found that it also gave her life a new sense of purpose. The initial months were clouded by confusion and grief, but eventually, a shift occurred. She could no longer deny that she had to do something more than simply live with myasthenia gravis—she wanted to help others who were going through similar challenges. Her struggles, once a source of despair, slowly began to feel like a platform for connection and advocacy.

It started one evening as Sarah sat in her living room, scrolling through social media, when she came across a post from a woman who had just been diagnosed with MG. The woman was scared and overwhelmed, much like Sarah had been. Reading through the comments, Sarah saw an outpouring of support from strangers across the world. Something clicked. Maybe she, too, could share her journey, not to seek pity, but to uplift others who felt lost and alone.

John, who had been working late in the kitchen, walked in and saw the look on Sarah's face. It was one he hadn't seen in a while—there was a spark, a light in her eyes.

"What's on your mind?" he asked, setting down a dish and sitting beside her.

Sarah didn't answer right away. Instead, she stared at her phone, deep in thought. "Do you remember when I was first diagnosed?" she asked quietly.

John nodded, his heart heavy with the memory. "I do."

"There was so much I didn't know, so much I was terrified to face," Sarah continued. "And I remember feeling so alone. But now, looking at these posts, these stories... I realize that I'm not the only one who's been through this. What if I could help someone the way others have helped me?"

John gave her a warm, encouraging smile. "You'd be great at that. You've got a lot to offer, Sarah. You've lived this, you understand it better than anyone."

Sarah hesitated, biting her lip. "But what if people think I'm just trying to get attention? I don't want to seem... selfish."

John shook his head firmly. "That's not you, Sarah. You're doing this for the right reasons, and anyone who knows you will see that. You've got a voice that people need to hear. You can offer hope."

Sarah's heart swelled with gratitude. It had been so long since she felt that she had something to offer the world. Slowly, she began to nod. "Maybe I could write about it. My journey, what I've learned... I'm not the same person I was before MG, but maybe that's okay. Maybe I can help someone else find their way through the darkness."

Finding Her Voice

The next morning, Sarah sat down at her desk, staring at the blank page in front of her. Her hands trembled slightly, a reminder of the physical limitations that now shaped her daily life. But she pushed the doubt aside and began to write.

The words didn't come easily at first. She struggled with how to express the depth of her emotions without sounding bitter or defeated. But the more she wrote, the more she realized that her journey wasn't just about the pain and the losses—it was also about the resilience she had found along the way. It was about the love and support of her family, the lessons she had learned, and the strength she had discovered in herself.

Her first post was simple. She shared her diagnosis story, her fears, and her hope for the future. She clicked "publish" and waited, unsure of what to expect.

Within hours, the comments began pouring in. Messages of encouragement, gratitude, and connection filled her inbox. Women and men from all over the world shared their own stories, thanking Sarah for her honesty and courage. Some had just been diagnosed, while others had been living with the disease for years. The sense of community was overwhelming, and for the first time in a long time, Sarah felt truly connected.

A New Routine

As the weeks went by, Sarah settled into a new routine. Each day, she would spend a few hours writing, responding to comments, and engaging with the online MG community. She began attending virtual support groups and even participated in a few podcasts, sharing her story with a wider audience.

One day, as she was sitting at her desk, typing away, Emily came into the room. "What are you working on?" she asked, peering over her mother's shoulder.

Sarah smiled, pushing a strand of hair behind her ear. "I'm writing a post about dealing with fatigue. It's something a lot of people with MG struggle with."

Emily nodded, sitting down next to her. "I think it's really cool that you're doing this, Mom. You're helping a lot of people."

Sarah looked at her daughter, her heart swelling with pride. "Thanks, sweetheart. It feels good to be able to do something that matters."

Emily bit her lip, her expression turning serious. "Do you ever feel scared about the future? You know, with your health?"

Sarah paused, her fingers hovering over the keyboard. It was a question she had asked herself many times, but hearing it from Emily made it feel more real. "Sometimes," she admitted softly. "But I try not to let it control me. I've learned that worrying about what might happen won't change anything. All I can do is live each day the best I can."

Emily nodded slowly. "I just... I don't want anything bad to happen to you."

Sarah reached out, pulling her daughter into a hug. "I know, sweetie. But no matter what happens, we'll face it together. We're a team, remember?"

Emily smiled through her tears. "Yeah, we are."

Spreading the Message

Sarah's journey didn't stop with blog posts and virtual groups. As her writing gained attention, she was invited to speak at a local MG awareness event. The idea of standing in front of a crowd, sharing her story, terrified her, but John and Emily encouraged her to take the leap.

"You've got this, Sarah," John said the night before the event. "Just speak from the heart. That's all anyone wants to hear."

The next day, standing in front of the microphone, Sarah took a deep breath. The faces in the audience blurred together, and for a moment, she wanted to turn and run.

But then she saw Emily in the front row, her eyes filled with pride, and something inside Sarah shifted.

"I was diagnosed with myasthenia gravis three years ago," Sarah began, her voice steady but soft. "At first, I thought my life was over. I couldn't see how I could continue living the way I used to. But over time, I realized that while MG changed my life, it didn't have to define me. I found strength in my family, in my community, and in myself."

She paused, looking out at the crowd. "I'm not here to tell you that living with a chronic illness is easy. It's not. But I am here to tell you that you're not alone. And if my story can help even one person feel less afraid, then it's worth sharing."

The room was silent for a moment before the applause began. Sarah's heart raced, but it wasn't fear this time—it was pride, joy, and a sense of purpose she hadn't felt in years.

A Legacy of Hope

As Sarah's involvement in advocacy grew, so did her influence. She started working with nonprofit organizations, helping to raise awareness and funds for MG research. Her voice, once timid and unsure, became a beacon of hope for those navigating the challenges of chronic illness.

One evening, after a particularly long day of meetings and writing, Sarah sat on the porch with John, a cup of tea in her hands. "I never thought my life would take this direction," she mused, staring out at the sunset.

John looked at her, his eyes filled with admiration. "You've made a difference, Sarah. You've touched so many lives."

Sarah smiled, her heart full. “I just hope I can keep going. There’s so much more to do.”

John reached over, taking her hand in his. “You’ve already done more than you know.”

As they sat together, the weight of the illness no longer felt so heavy. Sarah had found her new purpose, and with it came a sense of peace.

IX

Facing Setbacks

The steady hum of the hospital machines surrounded Sarah as she lay on the crisp white sheets, her body feeling heavier than usual. The familiar routine of medications, doctor visits, and tests had become part of her life, but this time it felt different. She had been dealing with myasthenia gravis for three years now, but something about this flare-up was more intense than anything she had experienced before.

John sat in the chair beside her, his hands clasped tightly in his lap. He looked older, more tired than he had in years past, as though Sarah's illness had aged him too. Emily had come by earlier, her usual energetic self noticeably subdued. It was clear that seeing her mother like this was taking a toll on her. Sarah hated that—hated the way her illness cast shadows over their lives, how it seemed to take up space that should have been filled with joy.

Dr. Martin walked into the room, holding Sarah's latest test results. His expression was serious, but he tried to soften it with a smile as he approached the bed. "How are you feeling today, Sarah?"

Sarah mustered a weak smile, though it didn't reach her eyes. "Tired. Really tired."

Dr. Martin nodded, glancing at her charts before speaking again. "Your latest test results show some increased muscle weakness. The flare-up you're experiencing right now is more severe than usual, and it's likely why you've been feeling more fatigued. We're going to need to adjust your treatment plan."

Sarah's stomach sank. She had been through this before—new medications, different dosages, and the constant adjustments to balance out the symptoms. It was exhausting. More than anything, she wanted her life back, but she knew that wasn't possible.

"How bad is it?" John asked, his voice tight with worry.

Dr. Martin hesitated before responding. "It's a significant setback, but not one we can't manage. With the right adjustments to her medications, we can get things under control again. But... it will take time. And Sarah will need to be careful. Overexertion could lead to further complications."

Sarah closed her eyes, trying to push down the rising wave of frustration. She had been careful. She had done everything she was supposed to do—resting when needed, taking her medications, and pacing herself. And yet, here she was, lying in a hospital bed, facing another setback. It felt like no matter how hard she tried, myasthenia gravis was always one step ahead, waiting to knock her down just when she thought she was getting back on her feet.

John reached over and took her hand, his grip gentle but steady. "We'll get through this," he whispered, though there was a tremor in his voice.

Sarah wanted to believe him, but it was getting harder. Every time she took a step forward, the disease pulled her two steps back. And she could see the toll it was taking on her family. Emily had started missing more school events, worried that her mother might need her at home. John worked longer hours, trying to balance his job with taking care of Sarah, and she could see the weariness in his eyes. They were all struggling, and the guilt weighed heavily on her chest.

That evening, after the doctors had come and gone, and the hospital halls had quieted down, Sarah stared out the window at the city lights in the distance. It was hard to imagine that life was still happening outside these walls—people going to work, having dinner with their families, living normal lives. Meanwhile, her world had shrunk to the size of this hospital room.

Emily came by after school, her backpack slung over one shoulder and a determined look on her face. She was always trying to be strong for her mom, even though Sarah could see the fear behind her eyes.

"Hey, Mom," Emily said, sitting down on the edge of the bed. "How are you feeling?"

"I've had better days," Sarah admitted, her voice tired.

Emily frowned, her fingers fidgeting with the strap of her backpack. "Is it bad? I mean... is it going to get better?"

Sarah sighed, unsure of how to answer. She didn't want to lie to her daughter, but the truth was hard to face. "It's a setback," she said finally. "But we'll get through it."

Emily nodded, though she didn't look convinced. "I hate this," she blurted out suddenly, her voice breaking. "I hate seeing you like this. I hate that you're sick. It's not fair."

Sarah's heart ached as she reached out to pull Emily into a hug. "I know, sweetie. I hate it too."

Emily buried her face in her mother's shoulder, her tears soaking into Sarah's hospital gown. "I just want things to go back to how they were," she whispered.

"I do too," Sarah whispered back, her own tears threatening to spill. "But we can't go back. We can only move forward."

The conversation left Sarah feeling emotionally drained, but it also reminded her of the strength of her family. They had been through so much already, and even though there were moments when it felt like they were barely holding on, they always found a way to get through it together.

Adjusting to the New Normal

The next few weeks were a blur of doctor's appointments, medication changes, and physical therapy sessions. Sarah's body was slow to respond, and the fatigue that had settled deep into her bones refused to lift. But she pushed through, determined to regain as much of her strength as she could.

John was a constant presence by her side, offering quiet support when she needed it most. He had always been the rock in their family, the one who held everything together even when it felt like things were falling apart. But Sarah could see the strain it was putting on him. Late at night, when he thought she was asleep, she would catch him sitting in the chair by the window, his head in his hands, the weight of the world on his shoulders.

One night, as Sarah lay in bed, staring up at the ceiling, she spoke into the darkness. "I'm sorry."

John looked up, startled. "For what?"

"For all of this. For everything this illness has done to us. To you and Emily. It's not fair."

John stood up and walked over to the bed, sitting down beside her. "None of this is your fault, Sarah," he said softly. "We're in this together. You didn't choose this. But I did choose to be here with you. And I wouldn't change that for anything."

Tears welled up in Sarah's eyes as she reached for his hand. "I just wish... I wish things were different."

"I know," John said, his voice thick with emotion. "But we'll make the best of what we have. We always do."

The Emotional Toll

Despite their best efforts to stay positive, the emotional toll of Sarah's illness began to take its toll on the family. Emily started acting out at school, her grades slipping and her once-bubbly personality becoming more withdrawn. Sarah knew that her daughter was struggling to cope, but there was only so much she could do from her hospital bed.

One afternoon, after another difficult therapy session, Sarah asked John to bring Emily in for a conversation. When Emily arrived, she looked sullen, her arms crossed over her chest as she stood at the foot of her mother's bed.

"Emily," Sarah began, her voice gentle but firm, "I know things have been really hard lately. For all of us."

Emily didn't say anything, but her expression softened slightly.

"I want you to know that it's okay to be angry. It's okay to be scared. But we need to talk about how you're feeling. You don't have to go through this alone."

Emily's eyes filled with tears as she finally met her mother's gaze. "I'm just... I'm scared, Mom. I'm scared that you're not going to get better. And I hate that I can't do anything to help."

Sarah's heart broke at her daughter's words, but she knew she had to stay strong for both of them. "I know, sweetheart. But I'm not going anywhere. We're going to get through this, one day at a time."

Emily wiped her eyes, nodding slowly. "Okay."

As they sat together, Sarah realized that the real battle wasn't just with her illness—it was with the fear and uncertainty that came with it. But she also knew that as long as they had each other, they could face whatever came their way.

X

Leaving a Legacy

The soft afternoon light filtered through the window, casting a warm, golden glow over the room. It was one of those moments where everything seemed to slow down, as if the world outside had paused to honor the fragility within. Sarah lay in bed, her body weakened by the years of fighting myasthenia gravis. Each breath was an effort, but she was determined to remain present, aware that the time left to say what mattered most was slipping through her fingers. The disease had taken so much from her—strength, energy, even moments with her family—but not her will to be there for the final chapter of her life.

John sat beside her, his hand gently holding hers, his thumb brushing across her knuckles in a rhythmic motion that had once soothed her. His face was etched with exhaustion, the wear and tear of years spent as a caregiver now showing clearly in the lines that crinkled around his eyes. Emily, their daughter, was curled up in the armchair near the window, watching her mother with a mixture of love and fear that had become all too familiar over the past few years.

"John," Sarah whispered, her voice barely audible but filled with a quiet strength that demanded attention.

He looked up from her hand, his heart aching at the sound of her voice. "What is it, Sarah? Do you need anything?"

She shook her head slowly, her lips curling into a small smile. "No, I just... I want to talk. I need to say some things while I still can."

John's throat tightened as he nodded, knowing what was coming. He had always dreaded this moment, the one where Sarah would confront the inevitable, where they would have to face the reality of what was about to happen.

Emily straightened in her chair, sensing the weight of the conversation. The air in the room seemed to grow heavier, the unspoken acknowledgment of what was coming pressing down on all of them.

Sarah turned her head slightly to look at her daughter. "Emily, sweetheart, come here."

Emily hesitated for a moment before standing up and walking over to the bed, sitting down on the edge beside her mother. She reached out and took Sarah's other hand, her fingers trembling as she held on tightly.

"I know this hasn't been easy," Sarah said softly, her voice filled with a tenderness that only a mother could offer. "You've had to grow up faster than most kids your age. You've had to face things no one should ever have to deal with."

Emily's eyes filled with tears, and she quickly wiped them away with the back of her hand, trying to stay strong. "Mom, don't... don't talk like that."

"I need to, Em. We need to talk about this." Sarah paused, her breath coming in short, labored gasps. "I'm so proud of you. You're strong. So much stronger than I ever was at your age."

"I'm not strong," Emily whispered, her voice cracking. "I hate this. I hate that you're sick. I hate that I can't do anything to help."

Tears welled up in Sarah's eyes as she heard the pain in her daughter's voice. "I know, sweetheart. But you've helped more than you realize. You've been there for me every step of the way, and that's more than enough."

Emily shook her head, her tears now falling freely. "But what am I supposed to do without you?"

John shifted uncomfortably, his own emotions threatening to spill over. He wanted to say something, anything to comfort his daughter, but he was at a loss. How could he reassure her when he didn't have the answers himself?

Sarah squeezed Emily's hand gently. "You'll do what you've always done. You'll keep going. You'll live your life. You'll follow your dreams, and you'll be happy. That's all I want for you, Em."

Emily nodded, though her heart felt like it was shattering into pieces. "I don't know if I can."

"You can," Sarah said firmly, her eyes locking onto her daughter's. "You're stronger than you think. And you'll have your dad. You'll have each other."

John leaned in closer, his voice thick with emotion. "We'll be okay, Em. We'll figure it out together."

Sarah smiled at both of them, her heart swelling with love. She reached into the bedside drawer and pulled out a small, worn leather journal, the pages filled with her handwriting, some of the ink smudged from tears shed during the late nights she spent writing in it.

"I started this for you both a while ago," Sarah said, handing the journal to Emily. "I wrote down everything I wanted to say—things about life, about love, about all the moments I wish I could be there for. I won't always be with you, but in some way, through this, I will."

Emily took the journal, her hands trembling as she clutched it to her chest. "Thank you, Mom."

Sarah nodded, a soft, tired smile spreading across her face. "Just promise me one thing, both of you. Promise me you'll live. Really live. Don't let my illness be the thing that holds you back. Use it as a reminder of how precious life is."

John and Emily nodded, their faces wet with tears. "We promise," they said in unison.

As the sun began to set outside, casting a soft, golden hue over the room, Sarah closed her eyes, feeling a sense of peace settle over her. She had said what she needed to say. She had given her family everything she had left to give.

In the quiet that followed, John and Emily sat with her, holding her hands, their hearts heavy with the weight of what was to come. They knew that while Sarah's body would soon be gone, her presence would remain with them—in their hearts, in their memories, and in the words she had written for them in her journal.

Sarah passed away peacefully that night, surrounded by the two people she loved most in the world. The next morning, as the sun rose over the horizon, casting its light on a world that felt infinitely emptier without her, John and Emily were left to face the overwhelming silence.

For days, the house felt hollow, as if the very walls had absorbed Sarah's absence. John wandered through the rooms, his hands brushing against the surfaces she had once touched, his mind replaying memories of their life together. Emily retreated into herself, spending hours in her room, clutching the leather journal to her chest but unable to open it, not yet ready to confront the words her mother had left behind.

It was a week later, during a quiet evening, that Emily finally sat down on the edge of her bed and opened the journal. Her hands shook as she flipped through the pages, her mother's familiar handwriting dancing across the lines. Each word felt like a whisper from Sarah, a message sent from a place beyond the pain and the loss.

John found her there, sitting cross-legged on the floor, the journal open in front of her, her tears falling silently onto the pages. He knelt beside her, wrapping his arms around her shoulders, holding her as she cried.

Together, they read through the journal, Sarah's words guiding them through their grief. She had written about the beauty of life, the importance of love, and the strength they would find in each other. She had left them stories, advice, and even silly little notes that made them smile through their tears.

In the months that followed, John and Emily found ways to honor Sarah's memory. They created a small garden in the backyard, planting her favorite flowers—lilies and lavender—so that her presence would always be with them. They took up activities she had loved, like baking and painting, keeping her spirit alive in the everyday moments.

Emily, inspired by her mother's resilience and the strength Sarah had seen in her, began writing in her own journal. She poured her heart into the pages, writing about her grief, her memories, and her determination to live the life her mother had wanted for her.

John, too, found solace in the journal. He would often sit outside in the garden, reading through Sarah's words, feeling her presence beside him. He knew that Sarah's legacy wasn't just in the journal she had left behind—it was in the love they had shared, the family they had built, and the strength they would carry forward.

Sarah had given them the greatest gift of all—the knowledge that love, even in the face of death, could endure. Her legacy lived on in their hearts, guiding them through the darkness, reminding them that life, even with its inevitable pain, was still worth living.

LEGACY OF LOVE

The soft hum of the wind rustling through the trees was the only sound that broke the stillness in the air. The small garden outside their home, once alive with Sarah's presence, now stood as a living testament to her resilience and love. It had been months since Sarah's passing, yet the weight of her absence was still fresh, as though time had paused in reverence for her memory.

John sat in the corner of the garden on the old wooden bench Sarah had always loved. His hands rested on his lap, and in them, he held her journal—the one she had gifted to Emily, full of the thoughts, wishes, and wisdom she wanted to pass on. He hadn't read it much since her death, partly because every word felt like a fresh wound, but today he felt an urge to connect with her once more.

He opened the journal to a random page, and there, in her familiar, graceful handwriting, was a note she had written for him:

"John, you have been my rock through every trial, every tear, and every moment of joy. I want you to know that even when I'm gone, I'm with you. You've given me the greatest gift—love that never wavered, even in the darkest of days. Please, live fully, the way you always encouraged me to. Don't let the weight of my illness take away your light. I'll always be watching over you and Emily. I love you more than words can say."

John swallowed hard as tears welled up in his eyes. He had been so focused on surviving the day-to-day without her that he had forgotten to truly live, just as Sarah had feared. The pain of her absence was so overwhelming at times that it felt impossible to move forward. But Sarah's words were a gentle reminder of the promise they had made—to live, even in her absence.

Just then, Emily came into the garden. She had grown so much in these past months, in ways John couldn't have imagined. She had taken on responsibilities with a maturity that belied her years, though there were moments where he saw the grief still raw behind her eyes.

She sat beside her father, curling her legs under her as she leaned against his shoulder. "Are you reading Mom's journal again?" she asked softly, noticing the familiar leather-bound book in his lap.

John nodded, his voice thick with emotion. "Yeah. I miss her."

Emily's eyes filled with tears, but there was also a quiet strength in her gaze. "I miss her too, Dad. Every day. But you know what? She's still with us. I feel it."

John turned to look at her, his brow furrowing. "How do you mean?"

Emily smiled through her tears, reaching into her pocket to pull out a small piece of paper. "I've been writing too," she confessed, handing the note to her father. It was a short letter, written in her neat handwriting, and as John read, his heart swelled.

"Dear Mom,

I miss you so much, and sometimes I feel lost without you. But I remember what you always said about living life to the fullest, no matter what. I want you to know that I'm trying. I'm trying to be strong, just like you. You fought so hard, even when the world seemed so unfair, and I want to live with that same strength. I promise I'll keep going, no matter what. I love you. Always."

John exhaled shakily, overwhelmed by pride and sadness. "Emily, that's beautiful," he whispered, pulling her into a tight embrace.

Emily clung to her father, her tears finally spilling over. "I don't want to let her down," she said, her voice trembling. "I want to make her proud."

John nodded, brushing a tear from his daughter's cheek. "You already have, Em. Every day, you make her proud."

The two of them sat there for a while, surrounded by the flowers Sarah had planted with so much care. The scent of lavender filled the air, and John could almost hear her voice, reminding them to keep going, to cherish life despite the pain.

Emily wiped her eyes and stood up, determination shining through her grief. "I've been thinking," she said, her voice steadier now. "We should do something to honor Mom's memory. Something that reflects the way she lived—how she never gave up, how she always helped others."

John looked up at her, curiosity piqued. "What do you have in mind?"

Emily's face brightened with the hint of an idea. "What if we started a foundation? For people with myasthenia gravis and other chronic illnesses. We could provide support, raise awareness, and share stories like Mom's. I think she'd like that."

John felt a warmth spread through his chest. It was as if Sarah was nudging them in the right direction, guiding them from wherever she was. "I think she'd love that," he said softly, feeling a sense of purpose begin to stir within him for the first time in months.

In the months that followed, Emily and John threw themselves into their mission. They named the foundation **"Sarah's Light,"** a beacon of hope for those battling chronic illness. It started small—just a few fundraisers and local support groups—but it quickly grew. People from all over reached out, sharing their own stories of resilience, inspired by Sarah's life and her unyielding spirit.

Through the foundation, Emily found a way to channel her grief into something positive. She became an advocate for those who felt unseen, just as her mother had during her battle with MG. Her speeches at events were filled with raw emotion, as she shared the lessons she had learned from her mother's journey.

"My mom taught me that life is precious, even when it's hard. She never gave up, even when her body did. She lived every moment with purpose, and that's something we all can learn from. Myasthenia gravis didn't define her; her love, her strength, and her spirit did. And I want to carry that forward for her."

John, too, found solace in his work with the foundation. Every event, every conversation with a patient or a caregiver, felt like a tribute to Sarah. He saw her in the smiles of the people they helped, in the strength of those who refused to let their illness define them. It was as if, through their work, they were keeping her alive, letting her light shine on even in the darkest of times.

Years passed, and though the pain of losing Sarah never truly left them, John and Emily found a way to carry it with grace. They learned to live with it, just as Sarah had taught them. They honored her by living fully, by laughing, by loving, and by never taking a single day for granted.

Sarah had left them with the greatest gift of all—a legacy of love, resilience, and hope. It was a legacy that would continue to inspire not only them but countless others for generations to come.

And in that legacy, Sarah's light would never fade.

www.ingramcontent.com/pod-product-compliance
Lightning Source LLC
LaVergne TN
LVHW041230150826
845673LV00008B/2338

* 9 7 9 8 8 9 5 8 8 0 4 7 0 *